The Lion and The Mouse

A Tale about Being Helpful

Retold by Sarah Price
Illustrated by Dennis Hockerman

Famous Fables

Reader's Digest Young Families

One day a little mouse discovered a patch of berries and began nibbling away. She spied a few especially large, juicy berries hanging from a branch just above a big rock. She scampered up the side of the rock and was just reaching for the nearest berry when the rock moved!

It was, in fact, not a rock at all. The little mouse discovered she had climbed up on the back of a sleeping lion! With a little squeak of fright, she started to scamper away. But the lion opened one eye and, quick as a wink, trapped her by her tail beneath his massive paw.

"Oh, please, do not eat me, Your Majesty!" she pleaded to the king of beasts. "I am but a tiny morsel to someone as great as you!"

The lion chuckled. "I have no intention of eating you, little mouse," he said. "You are too small to bother eating. But I am quite annoyed that you have woken me up from my nap. Why should I spare your life?"

The little mouse gave another squeak of fright. "Because it would be kind of you to let me go free," she replied, quivering. "Perhaps someday I shall have the chance to repay you for your kindness."

At this the lion roared with laughter. The idea that a creature as small as the little mouse could help someone as strong and mighty as he amused him so much that he lifted up his great paw and allowed the little mouse to run free.

A few weeks passed. Then one day the lion was searching for something to eat when he caught the scent of food in the breeze. He turned in the direction of the smell.

The lion took a step and suddenly felt a rope tighten around his paws. He had walked into a trap set by hunters! These hunters were trying to capture a live lion to bring back to the palace as entertainment for the king.

The lion thrashed furiously as he grew more and more entangled in the strong ropes.

But the more the lion struggled, the tighter his bonds grew. There was no hope of escaping. The lion roared with anger.

The little mouse heard the lion's roar. She could tell by the sound that the lion was in trouble. She scurried as fast as she could to reach him.

"Do you need help?" asked the little mouse.

The lion said to the mouse, "I am afraid there is nothing you can do for me."

"Yes, there is," said the mouse.

Little by little, one by one, the tiny mouse gnawed through the ropes that bound the huge lion, using her sharp little teeth. Soon she had freed one of the lion's paws and then another. After a while, the lion was able to wriggle out of the trap!

The lion was free!

"You see, Your Majesty," said the little mouse proudly, "sometimes a very little friend can be a very big help!"

"How right you are!" said the lion gratefully. "You are a very wise little mouse."

And from that day forward, the big lion and the tiny mouse were very close friends.

Famous Fables, Lasting Virtues
Tips for Parents

Now that you've read The Lion and The Mouse, *use these pages as a guide to teach your child the virtues in the story. By talking about the story's message and engaging in the suggested activities, you can help your child develop good judgment and character.*

About Being Helpful

Most children like to be helpful. When given the right opportunities to be helpful, children feel useful and proud of themselves. Realizing they can be helpful to others despite their small size—like the mouse in the story—boosts children's self-esteem and leads to future compassionate behavior. As parents, it is our job to teach our children different ways of helping others. Here are some ways to do so:

1. *Be a good example.* If you are helpful to others, your child will be, too. The more you demonstrate helpfulness, the quicker your child will learn it. Hold doors open for the person behind you. Give your seat on the bus to a person who seems to need it. Join in the cleanup after a friend's party. Help a neighbor weed the garden. When you do these small helpful acts, talk with your child about the importance of helping others without expecting anything in return.

2. *Make opportunities for your child to help out.* Ask for your child's help when sorting laundry, setting the table, or doing other household chores. Make helping out in your community a family activity—schedule time to perform easy, yet useful, tasks for seniors in your neighborhood. When there's news of a disaster that affects the lives of others, discuss how you and your family can help.

3. *Praise, praise, praise.* We often forget the importance of making positive statements to our children. Show your pleasure when your child performs a helpful act, no matter how small. When you praise your child's helpfulness, you are showing him how much you value his choices. They'll feel good about their actions and want to do them more often.